PUFFIN BOOKS

Mark Spark in the Dark

Jacqueline Wilson writes for children of all ages. *The Suitcase Kid* won the Children's Book Award, *Double Act* won the Smarties Prize, and *The Illustrated Mum* won the *Guardian* Children's Book of the Year Award.

Jacqueline lives near London in a small house crammed with 10,000 books.

Some other books by Jacqueline Wilson

For older readers

TAKE A GOOD LOOK
VIDEO ROSE
THE WEREPUPPY
THE WEREPUPPY ON HOLIDAY

Jacqueline Wilson

Mark Spark in the Dark

Illustrated by Bethan Matthews

PUFFIN BOOKS

PUFFIN BOOKS

Published by the Penguin Group
Penguin Books Ltd, 80 Strand, London WC2R 0RL
Penguin Putnam Inc., 375 Hudson Street, New York, New York 10014, USA
Penguin Books Australia Ltd, 250 Camberwell Road, Camberwell Victoria, Australia
Penguin Books Canada Ltd, 10 Alcorn Avenue, Toronto, Ontario, Canada M4V 3B2
Penguin Books India (P) Ltd, 11 Community Centre, Panchsheel Park,
New Delhi – 110 017, India
Penguin Books (NZ) Ltd, Cnr Rosedale and Airborne Roads, Albany,
Auckland, New Zealand
Penguin Books (South Africa) (Pty) Ltd, 24 Sturdee Avenue,
Rosebank 2196, South Africa

Penguin Books Ltd, Registered Offices: 80 Strand, London WC2R 0RL

www.penguin.com

First published by Hamish Hamilton 1993
Published in Puffin Books 1994
3

Text copyright © Jacqueline Wilson, 1993
Illustrations copyright © Bethan Matthews, 1993
All rights reserved

The moral right of the author and illustrator has been asserted

Made and printed in England by Clays Ltd, St Ives plc

British Library Cataloguing in Publication Data
A CIP catalogue record for this book is available from the British Library

This edition has been produced exclusively for Nestlé Cheerios and
Honey Nut Cheerios

ISBN 0-141-31532-6

Contents

Mark Spark

Chapter One

"Hands up all of you with a dog at home," said Miss Moss.

Mark's friend Jason put his hand up. Jason had a spaniel called Ben who had once eaten a whole box of chocolates in ten minutes flat. Louise from down the road had her hand up. Louise had a poodle called Puffball who whined a lot. Mark felt he would whine too if he had to wear a red ribbon and a silly tartan coat. That was no way to treat a dog. It

wasn't fair. Mark would have loved a
dog but he couldn't have one.

Mark's mum and dad were out at
work all day so there would be no
one to look after a dog. There was no
one to look after Mark when he came
home from school so Mark always
went round to Great Gran's for his
tea. Then he got another tea when
Mum came to fetch him home. Mark
was very nearly as greedy as Jason's
spaniel Ben.

"Tell me all the different things
your dogs can do," said Miss Moss.

"Jason's dog can eat heaps," said
Mark. "And then he's sick heaps
too."

"Mark Spark!" (He was really
called Mark Spencer, but everyone

called him Mark Spark. Even Miss Moss).

"And Louise's dog whines and whimpers like this," said Mark, imitating Puffball.

"*Mark Spark!*" said Miss Moss. "Give some of the others a chance to answer, please."

Mark slumped in his seat. He listened to the other children telling long stories about Woofer and Bruce and Rover. He wasn't impressed.

"So your dogs can fetch their own leads and open doors and bark at strangers. But I'm going to show you a picture of a very clever dog who can do something else. Something very important indeed," said Miss Moss.

4

Mark looked at the big picture
Miss Moss was holding. He saw a
cream labrador in a special harness
leading a woman with dark glasses.

"This lady's blind. She can't see at
all. Try closing your eyes for a
moment. Now imagine you've got to

get yourself out of the classroom, across the playground, out of the gate and all the way home without once opening your eyes. It would be very difficult, wouldn't it?"

Mark's eyes were open, not shut. He had his hand up and was bouncing around in his seat.

"I know what it's like, Miss. My Great Gran's blind. She can't go out, well, not much."

"Don't shout, Mark. It can't be easy to be your Great Granny. Now, this dog is a specially trained guide dog. He's leading the lady along, helping her safely across the road.

Guide dogs like this one do a wonderful job. But it takes lots of money to train them. Our school is going to try to raise enough money to train a special guide dog. Now, how can our class make some money?"

"I've got an idea, Miss," said Mark.

"Let's hear from someone else for a change," said Miss Moss. "Louise?"

"We could have a bring and buy sale, Miss Moss," said Louise. She liked bringing and was very good at buying.

"We could have a sponsored run," said Jason, who always came first at running.

"I've got a better idea," said

8

Mark, who simply couldn't keep quiet. "Let's have a parade with all of us dressed up as guide dogs with collecting tins round our necks and we could have my Great Gran at the back of the parade and we could be leading her. We could all go *woof*, *woof*, *woof* and —"

"That's enough, Mark. It's certainly an original idea but I don't think it's very practical. Still, I'm glad you're showing such an interest."

Chapter Two

No wonder Mark was interested. He boasted to Jason and Louise all the way home.

"Just wait till you see my Great Gran out with her guide dog! He'll have to go very slowly so my Great Gran can keep up. I'll train him to be ever so careful."

"Don't talk daft, Mark Spark," said Louise. "They have proper trainers for the guide dogs."

"And Miss Moss didn't say your

Great Gran was getting this guide
dog," said Jason.

"She's blind so of course she'll get
one," said Mark. "Wait till my Great
Gran hears."

"I think the whole street can
hear," said Jason, wincing away
from Mark. "You don't half bellow
sometimes, Mark."

Mark was used to talking in a loud voice for Great Gran because she was a little deaf as well as blind. She couldn't hear when Mark knocked at her door so he had his own key.

"*Great Gran!*" Mark yelled, flying through her hall.

Great Gran wasn't great at all. She was a very little lady and when Mark went bounding straight on top of her she nearly got squashed.

"What's this, the human whirlwind?" she said. "Get off of me, you great lump!" but she laughed and tickled Mark.

"D-o-o-o-n't!" Mark squealed. He was very ticklish, especially under the arms. "Give over, Great Gran. Listen!"

"I can't help but listen, Mr Squirm-and-Squiggle. You hungry? The teapot's brewing and there's marmite and crisp sandwiches and jammy buns."

"Wow, great. But do listen, Great Gran. You're going to get a dog!"

"No, I'm not!"

"Yes, you are. My school's saving up to get you a dog."

"What would I be doing with a dog at my age, you soppy date? I can't even get out myself, let alone take a dog for a walk."

"That's the point, Great Gran," said Mark, tucking into his tea. "You don't have to take the dog for a walk. It can take *you* for a walk. It's a guide

dog, get it?" Mark sprayed crisp crumbs in his excitement.

"Oh, one of them," said Great Gran. "Yes, they're a smashing idea. That young girlie I see up at the eye hospital, she's going to be getting a guide dog. It'll make all the difference to her. She'll be able to pop into the town or slip out of an evening no bother at all."

"But I want you to have a guide

dog, Great Gran!" said Mark, so
upset that he actually stopped eating.

"They'd never give me a guide
dog, pet. I'm too old. I couldn't get
out and about even if I had a dog.
And I'd have to be taught how to
look after it, and *I'm* too old a dog to
learn new tricks."

"Ooooh," said Mark, bitterly

16

disappointed. "Why do you have to be so old, Great Gran?"

"That's what I ask myself, little chum. Here, have a jammy bun. Have them both, darling, you're a growing boy."

Mark ate both buns and felt a bit better. They settled down in front of the television and watched *Neighbours* (Great Gran just listened) and then Mark read aloud. They were reading

from a big fat paperback called *Love's Flame*. They hadn't got to any flaming bits yet, but there was a lot of love. They were the bits Great Gran and Mark liked best. He read in funny voices, deep down in his tummy for Sir Jasper and high up and silly for Roseanne the servant girl. Great Gran laughed until her eyes went weepy. Mark laughed too and forgot about the guide dog.

Chapter Three

Mark still wanted to help raise the money for the guide dog all the same.

Miss Moss decided to try the Bring and Buy sale first.

"Bring lots of gifts," said Miss Moss.

Jason was bringing a big box of chocolates (if he could keep them out of Ben's way).

Louise was bringing a big plush teddy she'd never played with and some old videos and a knitted toilet roll cover made by her mum.

Mark had problems deciding what to bring. He wanted all his toys and his mum was too busy to make anything.

"I can knit," said Great Gran. "I'll knit you up a pair of socks quick as a wink."

"Thanks," said Mark doubtfully. Great Gran had never been much of a knitter even when she could see.

He felt even more doubtful when
she produced the socks. They were
made out of scraps of wool so they
didn't even match. One was mostly
pink, with yellow stripes. The other
was red with black at the top.

"Do they look all right?" said
Great Gran. "I think I might have
dropped a stitch or two."

"They look smashing," said Mark
loyally.

The other children didn't think
they looked smashing when he

slipped them on the Bring and Buy stall. They laughed and pointed.

"Whoever brought those awful old socks?" they said.

Jason knew. Louise knew. They looked at each other. They looked at Mark.

"I think they're absolutely brilliant socks," said Mark fiercely. "I've simply got to have them before anyone else snaps them up. Only thirty pence? That's a real bargain!"

He bought the socks himself. He put them on there and then, although they looked even odder on the leg. Mark only had five pence left to spend now. Nowhere near enough for the box of chocolates.

"Well, they'll keep your feet warm

anyway," said Jason.

"They look dead trendy," lied
Louise.

Mark smiled at his friends and
didn't mind quite so much about the
chocolates. And at least Great Gran's

socks weren't left lying unwanted on
the stall. Louise's mum's knitted
toilet roll cover was reduced right
down to five pence and still no one
would buy it. Louise was getting very
pink in the face.

24

"I'll buy it as a present for my Great Gran," said Mark. "I bet she'll like it."

Great Gran liked it a lot.

"What a dear little knitted hat. I'll pop it on every time I go out in the back yard. It'll keep my head nice and cosy."

Great Gran's socks kept Mark's
feet more than cosy. He wore them
when they had their sponsored walk.
(Miss Moss thought a run might
prove too energetic).

The walk seemed energetic enough
for Mark. Jason rushed ahead right
away. Then Louise left Mark far
behind. Soon Mark was trailing
round the playing fields by himself.

He sat down for a little rest. He

took his shoes off and aired his molten feet. One toe had poked a little hole in the red sock already. It looked like a nose peeping through. Mark wiggled his toe and made the sock stick its nose in the air. Then he made the sock sneeze. He'd have liked to play socks for the rest of the afternoon but he had to put his shoes back on and crawl round the playing field again. And again. And again. And even then he didn't do anywhere near as many circuits as Louise, let alone Jason. Left to Mark, they wouldn't manage as much as a puppy paw or the tip of a tail.

Chapter Four

"What am I going to do, Great Gran?" said Mark, munching a condensed milk sandwich. "I've been useless at this fund-raising lark so far. And now Miss Moss says our class are going to give a concert, charging ten pence a seat."

"That'll be fun, lovie," said Great Gran.

"No, it won't," Mark wailed, not watching his sandwich carefully enough. Condensed milk dripped

28

down his wrist and up his shirt
sleeve, so he had to lick it quickly.
"I don't know what to do in this
concert, Great Gran. Jason's going to
sing a pop song but Miss Moss says
I've got a voice like a fog horn.
Louise is going to do a ballet dance

and she's wearing a special fairy
costume but I can't dance for toffee."

"I can't see you being a fairy,
pet," said Great Gran. "Can't you
say a poem? You're ever so comic.
You always have me in stitches when
you read *Love's Flame*."

Mark thought hard, sticking his
finger into the jug of condensed milk
and then licking it. He did a lot of
sticking and licking. Sometimes it
was just as well Great Gran couldn't
see properly.

"Maybe we could act *Love's Flame*? I could get Louise to be Roseanne, only she'd try to do it properly and then it wouldn't be funny. Maybe Jason could be Roseanne? No, he'd feel soppy. *I'd* be Roseanne, only I've got to do Sir Jasper."

"Can't you do it all, pet? *I* know. Act it all out with puppets," said Great Gran.

31

"Yes! But how can I make puppets? I'm not much good at Art and Craft."

"You'll have to keep it simple. Glove puppets."

"Glove puppets," said Mark, and then he snapped his sticky fingers and grinned. "I've got an idea."

The concert was a big success. Jason sang his song. Louise did her ballet dance. Some of the boys

whistled when they saw her pink
ballet frock and Louise went pink
too, but she got on with her dance
and didn't wobble once. Then she
gave a fancy curtsey while everyone
clapped.

But the Mark Spark Puppet Show
was the smash hit of the concert. The
puppet booth was a big cardboard
box. Mark crouched down behind it
and stuck his hands up over the top,
working the two puppets. It made his
arms ache but he carried on
regardless. He spoke in Roseanne's
high squeaky voice while he made
the pink and yellow puppet prance.
(He'd simply sewn two blue button
eyes on the stripey sock and tied on a
hankie as an apron.) Then he spoke

34

in Sir Jasper's big booming voice and
made the red and black puppet
bounce about. (Two brown buttons
for his eyes and Mark's finger poking
through the hole made a perfect
nose.) Mark changed some of the
Love's Flame story, giving Sir Jasper a

terrible cold so that he could sneeze a
lot. He made the love scenes sillier
than ever, and every time the Sir
Jasper sock puppet pounced sneezily
on Roseanne, murmuring daft
endearments, the children roared
with laughter. Miss Moss looked a
little twitchy at first, but then she

started laughing too, and at the end
of Mark's performance she stood up
and cheered.

Mark had to act out the entire
puppet show at Great Gran's that
teatime, and she chuckled and clapped
and called him a proper caution, good
enough to go on the stage.

"That's what Miss Moss said, Great Gran," said Mark. "And guess what! She says I should do a puppet show in the playground every day and charge everyone a penny a time

to come and watch. I'm going to raise pounds and pounds for the guide dog."

Mark didn't quite raise pounds and pounds, but he certainly raised lots and lots of pennies. Eventually there was enough money to train a guide dog. The school was sent a big coloured photo of this very special dog. His name was printed at the bottom. He wasn't called Woofer or Bruce or Rover. He wasn't called Ben. He certainly wasn't called Puffball.

He was called Mark.

Mark Spark in the Dark

Chapter One

Mark Spark walked home from school with his friends Jason and Louise. It was raining hard. Jason was wearing his big black wellie boots. He stamped happily in every puddle. Louise was wearing her Kermit-the-frog wellie boots. She sloshed her way along the gutter, taking her twin Kermits for a paddle.

Mark Spark didn't have any wellie boots. Still, he didn't see why Jason and Louise should have all the fun.

43

He took a running jump at every puddle and landed with a big splash. He waded through the stream in the gutter and dabbled about in the sludge blocking the drains. His socks were soon sodden and his new trainers started to squelch.

"Your mum's going to get mad when she sees those trainers. You only had them on your birthday, didn't you?" said Jason.

"Mmm," said Mark, looking at his new trainers. They didn't look very new now. Jason was right. Mark's mum was going to get mad.

"I'm not frightened of my mum," said Mark, jumping in another puddle. He always had his tea with Great Gran, before Mum got back

from work. Maybe Great Gran could cook his trainers as well as his tea so they'd be dry by the time Mum saw them?

"I'm getting new trainers for my birthday too," said Louise. "Pink, to match my pink T-shirt and my pink leggings. Mark, come out of that puddle. Yuck, it's all gungy!"

Some of the gunge clung to Mark's trainers. He bent down to wipe it off. It moved. It was a big fat worm.

"Hello, worm!" Mark muttered. "What's your name, eh? I'm Mark Spark. And you're . . . Wilfred."

"Have you gone completely crackers, Mark?" said Jason. "Why are you talking to your trainers?"

"And for my best birthday present

46

I'm getting a tent. I want a pink one,
because it's my favourite colour,"
said Louise. "And my mum says for
my birthday treat I can have some
friends to stay over night and we can
all sleep in my tent out in the garden.
Won't that be great?"

"You bet!" said Jason. "We can
come, can't we, Mark and me? We're
your friends, aren't we, Mark?"
Suddenly he noticed that Mark was
holding something. "What's that
you've got in your hand?" he asked.

47

"It's my new pet. Say how do you do to Wilfred." Mark held Wilfred up so he could maybe waggle his tail.

"YUCK!" Louise squealed, and she went flying down the road in her frog wellies.

She screamed so loudly that Mark jumped and dropped Wilfred back in the puddle.

"Oh Wilfred, come back!" said Mark. "Louise, you are a bore. You've made Wilfred run away."

Louise was still running away herself. "You keep that horrid worm away from me," she shrieked. "If you bring it anywhere near me again I won't let you stay overnight in my tent."

"It's okay, Louise," said Jason,

dashing backwards and forwards between them. "He's dropped his worm. So we can still sleep in your tent, eh?"

"Bye bye, Wilfred," said Mark sadly, stirring the muddy puddle in vain.

"Don't you dare fetch it out again!" Louise shouted.

"I can't. You've frightened him away," said Mark, sighing. He squelched along the road. "I don't know why you don't like worms, Louise. They're your favourite colour. Pink."

"Is your birthday tent really going to be pink, Louise?" asked Jason.

"Yep, with a pink sleeping bag to match. You and Mark will have to bring your own sleeping bags for my birthday treat," said Louise.

"No problem," said Jason.

Mark Spark didn't say anything. He did have a little problem. No, not a little problem. A Great Big Problem.

Chapter Two

Mark Spark didn't know what he
was going to do. He didn't say
anything to Jason. He didn't say
anything to Louise. He couldn't tell
them about his Great Big Problem.
They might laugh at him. They
would think he was a silly baby. Just
thinking about it made Mark blush
Louise's favourite colour.

Mark Spark had always had this
Great Big Problem but he had kept it
a deadly secret so far. Mark Spark

was afraid of the dark.

He wasn't frightened of anything else. He'd dare anything. He didn't care about getting into trouble. He didn't cry when he fell and gashed his head and had to have ten stitches at the hospital. He didn't flinch when a pit bull terrier barked and tried to bite him. Everyone thought Mark Spark was the bravest boy in the whole school.

But he was still scared of the dark. He had a little lamp at home. Mum always left the hall light on too, in case he had to nip to the bathroom in the night. But even in the light he knew the dark was there, in all the other rooms. It was outside the windows, this huge terrifying darkness.

He knew he'd never be able to sleep outside in a tent with Jason and Louise. He could have a torch but that would be just a very little light in the very big darkness outdoors. It would be much much much too scary. Mark Spark might end up blubbing like a baby.

Great Gran guessed something was wrong when Mark went to her house for his tea.

"I've mucked up my new trainers, Great Gran," said Mark.

Great Gran was blind so she couldn't see them. But she could feel them.

"You mucky pup," she said. "We'd better give them a good wash, eh?"

Great Gran sorted out Mark's trainers as best she could.

"But there's still something wrong, duck," she said. "Can't you tell your Great Gran?"

"Well, I lost my pet worm Wilfred coming home from school," said Mark.

"Did you, dearie? How tragic," said Great Gran. "Still, I dare say you'll find yourself another worm. You could go out in my back garden and get one right away. How about a lady worm this time? Wilma Worm?"

"Yes, good idea, Great Gran," said Mark, but he didn't sound enthusiastic.

"There's still something bothering

my little lad," said Great Gran, and
she reached out for Mark and pulled
him onto her lap. "What is it,
chum?"

"Oh Great Gran!" Mark wailed.
"I don't know what to do. Louise is
getting a tent for her birthday and
she's asked me and Jason to stay
overnight to camp in her garden and

I can't because . . . because . . .
because I'm scared of the dark."
Mark said it in a very little voice.
Great Gran was rather deaf as well
as blind but she heard him and she
hugged him tight.

"Don't you fret yourself, my pet.
We'll sort something out, just you
wait and see."

Chapter Three

"I'm ever so sorry, Louise," said
Mark. "I really wish I could stay
overnight for your birthday treat.
But I can't. I've got to go and stay
with my Great Gran that weekend."

"Oh Mark!" said Louise,
frowning. "Don't muck up my
birthday treat."

"Can't you go and stay with your
Great Gran some other weekend?"
said Jason. "You've *got* to come too,
Mark."

"I'm sorry. But I've got to be with Great Gran. She's – she's scared of the dark, you see. She needs me there," said Mark.

"Hang on," said Jason. "Your Great Gran's blind, so she's always in the dark. Why should she be scared?"

Mark Spark scratched his head. "Burglars," he said. "There've been several break-ins down near my Great Gran's. She's getting nervous."

It was true enough. There had been several burglaries. And Great Gran *was* worried about it. And Mark Spark certainly wanted to look after her. Great Gran always looked after him. It was her idea that he should stay with her, so he needn't go to stay with Louise.

"It won't be any fun without you, Mark," said Jason.

"Yes it will," said Louise crossly. "Okay then, Mark. If you can't come I'll invite my friend Lily instead."

"Yuck! Not *Lily*," said Jason,

looking horrified. "I can't stick Silly Lily."

Jason didn't ever dare call Lily Silly to her face. She might have a small soft name but she was a big tough girl and she never let any of the boys boss her about. But she could be good fun too. She often had good ideas. Almost as good ideas as Mark Spark.

It was very hard for Mark listening to Louise and Jason and Lily planning the birthday treat.

"Mum says we can cook food on her little camping stove," said Louise.

"Sausages! Wow, can we have sausages?" said Jason.

"And if I bring my mum's special pan we could have pancakes with maple syrup," said Lily.

Mark's mouth was watering. It sounded as if the birthday treat was going to be such fun.

"Look, Louise, maybe I could come for the camp stove feast?" he said hopefully. "Then I could go along to my Great Gran's after, when it gets dark and you lot go to bed in the tent."

"No, Mum says I can only have two friends. She says more will just get silly. And now I've asked Jason and Lily," said Louise.

"Lily *is* silly," Jason muttered to Mark. "Hey, I do wish you were coming instead of her, Mark."

"So do I," said Mark miserably.

It was hard when he knew he wasn't going because *he* was the silly one.

Chapter Four

"We'll have our own camp fire feast,
little pal," said Great Gran on
Saturday night.

Mark helped her cook it in the
kitchen. They had sausages. They
had bacon too. And baked beans.
And chips. They didn't eat it at the
kitchen table as usual. They went
into Great Gran's lounge and she
switched her electric fire on, even
though it was a hot evening.

"It's our camp fire, right?"

said Great Gran.

"You bet," said Mark, sitting down cross-legged in front of the fire.

Great Gran couldn't quite manage to sit cross-legged, but she drew her armchair up near the fire and they had their feast. Then they had their pudding.

"Oh Great Gran!" said Mark, seeing the bowl of batter. "Are we having pancakes too?"

"You bet," said Great Gran.

She cooked the pancakes in very hot fat. They made a lot of smoke. It was very like a camp fire. Great Gran couldn't see but somehow she knew exactly when to toss each pancake. She made six. She ate two. Guess who ate four. One with lemon and sugar. One with jam. One with chocolate spread. And one with condensed milk.

Mark Spark felt very full indeed afterwards. He watched television with Great Gran but the heat from the fire and the food in his tummy made him feel very very sleepy.

"Come on, we're both nodding off," said Great Gran. "Let's go to bed, eh?"

They got undressed and Mark cleaned his teeth and Great Gran popped hers in an old cup in the bathroom. Then they both climbed into Great Gran's bed.

"We can play tents in here," said Great Gran, pulling the bedclothes

over their heads.

"No, it's a bit too dark, Great Gran," said Mark.

"Okay pet," said Great Gran, tucking the sheets back under Mark's chin.

She said Mark could keep the light on all night long. Mark snuggled up happily, feeling safe. Great Gran was especially cuddly without her corsets. Mark fell asleep straight away.

He had a funny dream about Louise and Jason and Lily. They were all safe in their tent with torches but they'd pushed him out in the dark and he didn't know what to do. He stumbled around in his dream, bumping into things and crying. He heard himself wailing and then he heard Great Gran's voice.

He woke up. He felt for Great Gran. He sat straight up in bed. Great Gran wasn't there! He heard the weird wailing again. And then he heard Great Gran's voice outside, down in the garden.

What was she doing out there in the dark by herself?

Mark started shivering, wishing Great Gran would come back. Then he heard a thump and a bang and a fumble and a groan. Great Gran!

Was it a burglar? Had he hurt Great Gran?

"You leave my Great Gran alone!" Mark Spark shouted, and he hurtled out of bed, out of the bedroom, down the stairs three at a time, down the passage and out the back door. Into the dark. The great black terrifying outdoor dark.

"Great Gran!" Mark shouted, scarcely able to see a thing. And then he bumped right into someone and shrieked.

"Hey, little darling, it's only me," said Great Gran, holding him tight. "What are you doing out in the garden, eh?"

"What are *you* doing out in the garden?" Mark gasped. "Where's the burglar?"

"There's no burglar, sweetheart. Just a silly cat who's been rooting around in my dustbin. I just tripped right over it. But I think we've frightened him off now."

"Good."

"So you thought there was a burglar? And yet you came out here in the dark to protect your old Great Gran, eh? That was very very brave of you."

Mark thought about it. "Mmm. Yes. I suppose it was," he said, pleased.

"The dark isn't so very terrible, is it?" said Great Gran.

Mark looked all around him. It wasn't so bad now he was holding Great Gran's hand. It wasn't really so frightening at all. It wasn't even as black as he'd expected. Maybe he'd be able to stay over at Louise's house next time.

He looked up at the dark sky and smiled.

"I can see all the stars, Great Gran," he said. "They sparkle."

"Like you, pet. My Markle Sparkle," said Great Gran.

Choosing a brilliant book
can be a tricky business...
but not any more

www.puffin.co.uk

The best selection of books at your fingertips

So get clicking!

Searching the site is easy – you'll find what you're looking for at the click of a mouse, from great authors to brilliant books and more!

Psst!
What's happening?

sneakpreviews@puffin

For all the inside information on the hottest new books,

click on the Puffin

www.puffin.co.uk

Read more in Puffin

For complete information about books available from Puffin – and Penguin – and how to order them, contact us at the appropriate address below. Please note that for copyright reasons the selection of books varies from country to country.

www.puffin.co.uk

In the United Kingdom: Please write to Dept EP, Penguin Books Ltd,
Bath Road, Harmondsworth, West Drayton, Middlesex UB7 ODA

In the United States: Please write to Penguin Putnam Inc., P.O. Box 12289,
Dept B, Newark, New Jersey 07101–5289 or call 1–800–788–6262

In Canada: Please write to Penguin Books Canada Ltd,
10 Alcorn Avenue, Suite 300, Toronto, Ontario M4V 3B2

In Australia: Please write to Penguin Books Australia Ltd,
P.O. Box 257, Ringwood, Victoria 3134

In New Zealand: Please write to Penguin Books (NZ) Ltd,
Private Bag 102902, North Shore Mail Centre, Auckland 10

In India: Please write to Penguin Books India Pvt Ltd,
11 Panscheel Shopping Centre, Panscheel Park, New Delhi 110 017

In the Netherlands: Please write to Penguin Books Netherlands bv,
Postbus 3507, NL–1001 AH Amsterdam

In Germany: Please write to Penguin Books Deutschland GmbH,
Metzlerstrasse 26, 60594 Frankfurt am Main

In Spain: Please write to Penguin Books S. A., Bravo Murillo 19,
1° B, 28015 Madrid

In Italy: Please write to Penguin Italia s.r.l.,
Via Felice Casati 20, I–20124 Milano

In France: Please write to Penguin France S. A.,
17 rue Lejeune, F–31000 Toulouse

In Japan: Please write to Penguin Books Japan, Ishikiribashi Building,
2–5–4, Suido, Bunkyo-ku, Tokyo 112

In South Africa: Please write to Longman Penguin Southern Africa (Pty) Ltd,
Private Bag X08, Bertsham 2013